Dear Parent:
Your child's love of reading starts here!

Every child learns to read in a different way and at his or her own speed. Some go back and forth between reading levels and read favorite books again and again. Others read through each level in order. You can help your young reader improve and become more confident by encouraging his or her own interests and abilities. From books your child reads with you to the first books he or she reads alone, there are I Can Read Books for every stage of reading:

SHARED READING
Basic language, word repetition, and whimsical illustrations, ideal for sharing with your emergent reader

BEGINNING READING
Short sentences, familiar words, and simple concepts for children eager to read on their own

READING WITH HELP
Engaging stories, longer sentences, and language play for developing readers

READING ALONE
Complex plots, challenging vocabulary, and high-interest topics for the independent reader

I Can Read Books have introduced children to the joy of reading since 1957. Featuring award-winning authors and illustrators and a fabulous cast of beloved characters, I Can Read Books set the standard for beginning readers.

A lifetime of discovery begins with the magical words "I Can Read!"

Visit www.icanread.com for information
on enriching your child's reading experience.

I Can Read® and I Can Read Book® are trademarks of HarperCollins Publishers.

The Good Egg and the Talent Show
Text copyright © 2022 by Jory John
Illustrations copyright © 2022 by Pete Oswald
Interior illustrations by Saba Joshaghani in the style of Pete Oswald
All rights reserved. Printed in the United States of America.
No part of this book may be used or reproduced in any manner whatsoever without written permission except
in the case of brief quotations embodied in critical articles and reviews. For information address
HarperCollins Children's Books, a division of HarperCollins Publishers, 195 Broadway, New York, NY 10007.
www.icanread.com

ISBN 978-0-06-295458-9 (pbk.)
ISBN 978-0-06-295459-6 (trade bdg.)

The artist used pencil sketches scanned and painted in Adobe Photoshop
to create the digital illustrations for this book.

23 24 25 26 CWM 10 9 8 7 6

First Edition

THE GOOD EGG
and the Talent Show

THEATER

THE TALENT SHOW   3:00PM

TICKETS

Written by Jory John

Cover illustration by Pete Oswald

Interior illustrations by Saba Joshaghani based on artwork by Pete Oswald

HARPER

An Imprint of HarperCollinsPublishers

I'm a good egg.

A very good egg.

Yes, a verrrrrrrrrrrrrry good egg.

And I have a problem.

A big problem.

Yes, a verrrrrrrrrrrrrry

big problem.

See, there's a talent show
this afternoon.

But I don't have any talents.

It's true.

I can't dance.

I don't know how to juggle.

I never sing in tune.

I don't have an ACT!

Meanwhile, everybody from the store

will be here.

All of them have amazing skills.

The pasta does yoga.

The cookies perform magic.

The marshmallows stack themselves
into tall towers.

The English muffins are actors.

The popcorn jumps REALLY high.

And the cheese plays

in a six-piece string band.

11

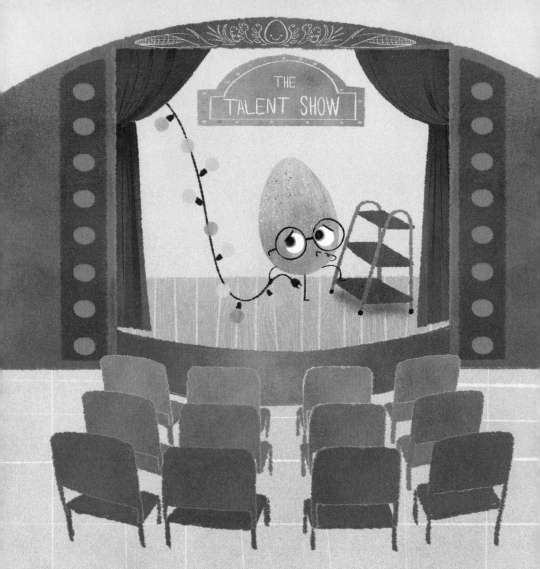

But I'm just a good egg.

Where are all MY amazing skills?

What are MY unique talents?

What am I even DOING with my life?

Think, Egg! Think!

What should I do?

What will I do?

What could I do?

The talent show is starting!

And I STILL don't have an act.

I guess I'll just sit in the audience

and cheer on my friends.

That's what I usually do anyway.

How can I compete with this?

I could never do something like that. . .

15

THE
TALENT SHOW

"ummm . . . .
. . . . . err"

Uh oh, that muffin seems
to have forgotten his lines.

16

Fortunately, I can help.

Sheggspeare is my favorite.

Oh dear.

No one is volunteering

for this magic act.

"Ooh, ooh, I'll do it!"

Goodness, that pose looks dangerous.
I should probably be a spotter.

Oh no, the drummer broke her drums.

Fortunately, I have my lucky bottle cap.

"Drum away, my new friend!"

Oh gosh, the lighting is all wrong.

And one of the costumes ripped.

Good thing I brought this flashlight

and this emergency sewing kit.

Wow, what a show!

That was the best one yet!

It's too bad I didn't get

to perform an act.

But I still had fun.

I was about to leave the theater
when something strange happened.
The string cheese asked me
to wait for a minute.

Everyone started saying

thank you—to me!

They said I made every act better.

The English muffin called me

the star of the show.

25

They were so grateful!

They couldn't believe
I'd set up this entire talent show
by myself.

They all said I was a good egg!

A verrry good egg.

That made me feel
verrry good, indeed.

Wow, that was really something.

I made some new friends and

I discovered some new talents.

And I learned an even bigger lesson:

People notice when you do good things.

Hmm. I guess being kind is a talent, too!

Yes, this was a good day

for a good egg, indeed.

I suppose I have some

useful skills, after all.

Whoa, another talent show

is coming up fast . . .

What will I do?

What shall I do?

What *could* I do?

Think, Egg! Think!